D1021122

Infiltration

Infiltration

Sean Rodman

orca soundings

ORCA BOOK PUBLISHERS

Library and Archives Canada Cataloguing in Publication

Rodman, Sean, 1972-
Infiltration / Sean Rodman.
(Orca soundings)

Issued also in electronic formats.
ISBN 978-1-55469-986-5 (bound).--ISBN 978-1-55469-985-8 (pbk.)

I. Title. II. Series: Orca soundings
PS8635.O355I54 2011   JC813'.6   C2011-903433-6

First published in the United States, 2011
Library of Congress Control Number: 2011929404

Summary: Bex breaks into locked and abandoned buildings
just because he can, but when a new friend's behavior becomes
more and more risky, he has to do the right thing.

*Orca Book Publishers is dedicated to preserving the environment and has printed
this book on paper certified by the Forest Stewardship Council®.*

Orca Book Publishers gratefully acknowledges the support for its publishing
programs provided by the following agencies: the Government of Canada
through the Canada Book Fund and the Canada Council for the Arts,
and the Province of British Columbia through the BC Arts Council
and the Book Publishing Tax Credit.

Cover photography by iStockphoto.com

ORCA BOOK PUBLISHERS
PO Box 5626, Stn. B
Victoria, BC Canada
V8R 6S4

ORCA BOOK PUBLISHERS
PO Box 468
Custer, WA USA
98240-0468

www.orcabook.com
Printed and bound in Canada.

14 13 12 11 • 4 3 2 1

To Laura

Chapter One

I don't recommend breaking and entering on your first date. Wait until you can really trust them. Asha and I waited in the shadows of a closed convenience store. We sized up the building across the street. The cold drizzle was starting to soak us. She squeezed my hand and kissed my cheek.

"Bex, this is going to be awesome," she said.

It was kind of romantic, I guess. We were looking over at the old Orpheus Theater. It was a tall, narrow building tucked between two ancient store-fronts. A tall neon sign crawled up the front of it, reading *ORPHEUS*. Smaller signs covered the ticket booth. A couple of big ones were marked *Closed* and *Demolition Order*.

The April rain made me wish I had brought more than my black hoodie. We needed to get moving or we'd get uncomfortable. I checked to make sure the coast was clear. At this time of night, there was barely any traffic. Most people with any sense were tucked into bed. But we were just getting started.

At my signal, Asha and I ran across the street. We headed straight into a narrow alley next to the Orpheus. We were on our way to meet up with my best friend Jake. We wanted to see what the theater looked like on the inside.

My friends and I have a hobby. We like to explore old buildings in the city. But not on the official tour. We go where we're not supposed to. In my opinion, a No Trespassing sign just means you're on your own. We're not the only ones. There's a bunch of people in the city who do this. They call themselves urban explorers. We compare notes and brag about our illegal adventures online. It's all anonymous, of course. On the urban exploration forums, I'm Urbex604. My real name is Taylor Bexhill. My friends just call me Bex.

It's a bit like being a superhero. In real life, I'm under the radar and keep to myself. I've never been into team sports. Never been cool enough to be part of the in crowd. As an urban explorer, though, I'm like a rock star. I've hacked more buildings in this city than almost anyone else. I look for old tunnels or abandoned buildings that nobody else can get into. Then I post some pictures from the inside. I've got a great slideshow of conquests now. The Orpheus Theater was one of the toughest sites in town. It had no easy entrances and some serious security guards. Now it was slated to be destroyed in a couple of weeks. I wanted to claim this one for my own before it went.

Don't get me wrong when I talk about breaking and entering. I'm not a criminal. I do this for fun. For bragging rights. I take nothing but pictures, leave nothing but footprints. Asha says that I act like a cross between a Boy Scout and a young offender. I pulled her into urban exploration a little while ago. She totally got into it. Which was a bit of a surprise to me. She's from a pretty strict family and comes across as really straight. But I'm not complaining.

Jake was waiting halfway down the alley. He stayed in the shadows as we got closer. He was dressed like us—black hoodie, black jeans, work boots, backpack. Jake could never really pull off the urban ninja look though. With his baby face, he looked a lot younger than seventeen. Especially when he smiled.

"Glad you two made it. I thought you might head to a real movie theater and leave me in the rain," he said.

"And let you to be the first one to crack the Orpheus? Dude. Bex might be my boyfriend, but he's not worth missing this for," Asha said. Jake laughed. I pulled a crowbar from my backpack and made a face at her.

Jake and I looked at the big manhole in the middle of the alley. "You sure this is it?" he asked. I nodded. I was pretty certain that this was our ticket inside. There was a network of old tunnels underneath these streets that led into the theater.

I'd read that when the Orpheus was built back in the 1920s, it was too hot inside during the summer. So the theater owners built tunnels to bring in air from the outside. Sometimes they actually put ice in the tunnels to cool down the air. I'd spent a few afternoons looking at blueprints in the city archives. I figured that the tunnels were probably still there but sealed off. Like I said, I'm all about research and planning. It's my secret power.

It took us a few minutes, but we got the manhole cover off. We even did it without a lot of noise. Asha was on lookout, but nobody was out in the rain.

Jake was first into the manhole. He flicked his headlamp on just before he disappeared. Asha was next, then me.

The tunnel was lined with crumbling old brick. It was drier than I would have expected in this weather. We tried to move quickly but had to duck. The ceiling was just a little too short for us to stand up in. The light from our headlamps bobbed around the tunnel.

After a few minutes, Asha turned to me. "Are you sure you know where we're going? It seems like we've gone too far," she whispered.

"It's all good. This is totally to plan," I lied. I was pretty sure we should have found a ladder going up by now. "We better catch up to Jake."

A couple of minutes later, Jake pointed his lamp at the ceiling. Sure enough, there was a rusted ladder rising into the darkness.

"Bex, you get the honor," said Jake. "This was your idea." He bowed a little and gestured up the ladder. I returned the bow and started climbing. The ladder felt a little funny with my weight on it. I hoped it would last long enough for all of us to get up.

Reaching the top, I hooked one arm through a rung. I pulled the crowbar from my backpack again. The top of the ladder ended against a bunch of wooden planks. It looked like I'd have to pry up some of them to get through. I kept my head turned away as the wood splintered apart. Then the ladder let loose a small metal squeal and I stopped. I looked down. It was a good fifteen-foot drop to where Jake and Asha were. I wouldn't die, but I might break something. The ladder groaned again. I needed to either get down or get through the planks, fast.

I decided to go through. I squeezed the crowbar deep in between two planks and shoved it with all my strength. The plank cracked upward just as the ladder popped away from the wall. I scrambled and got both arms through the new hole above me. That left my legs dangling in the air, tangled in the now-useless ladder. Sweat stung my eyes. I could feel my arms start to shake as they held my full weight. Asha called my name from down below. I heard Jake tell her to stay quiet.

Slowly, I inched up through the hole that I had made. Wiggling my legs, I got away from the ladder. Finally, I gave one big heave and yanked myself out of the tunnel. I rolled onto my back, breathing heavily. My headlamp barely illuminated the ceiling. It looked like it was maybe forty feet up. What I saw up there made me hold my breath. Then I scrambled back to the hole. I called down to Asha and Jake.

"You're not going to believe this," I said. "We get pictures of this online, and we'll be freaking famous."

Chapter Two

I was rushing, but it still took a couple of minutes to drop a climbing rope down to the others, then get them up to the stage. Finally we stood together with our headlamps sending little slivers of light across the gigantic hall. The wooden floorboards creaked as Jake started to walk around, exploring. Ranks of red seats rose away from the stage into the darkness.

I imagined hundreds of people in the audience, dressed up for a night at the theater.

But it was the ceiling that kept catching my eye. It was covered with a huge mural, a gigantic painting of ancient gods or something. Jake took some pictures. Even the bright light from his camera flash seemed tiny in the cavernous space. I pulled Asha closer to me and pointed up at the mural.

"This is why I do it."

"What do you mean?" she asked.

"Why I do this…what we do. The exploring. I like finding hidden treasures that are right in front of everyone. Beautiful things that most people take for granted." I looked at her as I said it. I didn't mean to sound smooth, but it kind of worked out that way. She gave me a little smile.

"That's pretty sweet, Bex."

I decided to seize the opportunity. I leaned in for a kiss. But before we connected, I heard Jake swear and I froze. I looked in his direction and saw the problem. The bright beam of a flashlight was pointed right at us.

"Hold it!" a deep voice barked out from the shadows.

A guard.

We scrambled back toward the hole that I'd ripped through to the stage. Jake got there first and dropped down the rope into the tunnel. Then I held the rope steady as Asha descended. By the time I was climbing backward down the hole, the guard was close. Too close. I let the rope slither fast through my hands and winced as I felt my fingers burn.

With a thump, I hit the tunnel floor and rolled. Jake and Asha helped me up. Then we were moving fast through the tunnel, our footsteps echoing loudly in the tunnel. But the guard didn't stand a chance of catching us.

By the time we were back on the street, we were still hyped on adrenaline. All the way to the bus stop, we kept laughing and retelling the best bits of our adventure. All that adrenaline eventually crashed out of us. On the long bus ride back toward our neighborhood, I just felt tired and hollow. Asha was asleep on my shoulder. Jake was snoring too, his head against the bus window.

The city at night scrolled by outside. I imagined we were floating along, sealed in a glass bubble. A perfect bubble. I had an awesome girlfriend. My best friend always, always had my back. I was even doing all right at school. And at night I was a superhero, able to go where no one else could. I didn't want anything to change.

I still had that feeling the next day when I met up with Asha again. We were in the first-period biology class at school. I'd first met Asha when she was assigned as my lab partner. Things had worked out pretty well. We'd been together for a couple of months now.

I was good at the textbook part of biology. But I don't have a high tolerance for gross. Asha, on the other hand, watched splatter films for fun. She wanted to go to med school and be a doctor. The dissection we were working on was particularly nasty, so she took the lead on it. Some sort of reptile was staked to a tray in front of us.

"Pass me the scalpel," she said. She smiled a little as she began carving away at the thing in front of us. I carefully kept my eyes on her and away from the green goo.

"Bex, you are such a wuss," she said without looking away from her work.

There was a squelching sound from inside the thing's body cavity. Ugh.

"Hey, I can be brave. I'm good at dark tunnels. Spiders, totally fine," I said. "Just not slimy dead things."

"Whatever," she said. She paused to pin down a flap of reptile skin. " So I heard back from Camp Kinnikee."

"Okay," I said. "Was that the one up in the mountains or on the coast?"

"The mountains. Turns out they decided to give me the head camp counselor job!" She waited for me to get all excited. When I didn't, she seemed a little thrown. She started speaking faster. She still didn't look at me.

"Here, hold the tray for me. Anyways, the pay is way better than what I could make working at the café. I'll make over four thousand dollars."

My stomach was squirming, and it wasn't the dissection that was bugging me.

"I won't even have to spend money on food 'cause we eat in the cafeteria at the camp," she kept going. "And because it's in the middle of nowhere, I won't be tempted to spend any money on movies or whatever. I'll have my tuition saved in no time."

Money was a big deal to her right now. I knew that Asha's parents had made it clear to her that if she wanted to go to university, she needed to work to raise the cash.

"So you took the job?" I said.

Asha finally put down the scalpel and looked at me. Her brown eyes locked on mine.

"It's not for too long, Bex. It's just a couple of months. Maybe two and a half."

"So you took it." I wanted to be happy for Asha, I really did. But there was no way I could be happy about a summer away from her. Suddenly I felt awkward and nervous. Asha finally put down her tools and looked at me. Her face was serious. Oh, crap. It hit me.

Was this her way of breaking up with me? Was she going away just to get rid of me?

There was a knock on the classroom door, and everyone in the class looked over. That's when the new kid walked in. He had long blond hair in a pony-tail and wore a black T-shirt with baggy camo pants. Mr. Kurtzia, the teacher, introduced him.

"Everyone, this is Kieran Ridgeway." Kieran looked edgy, like he wanted out of the spotlight.

Jake leaned back from the row in front of me.

"I heard about this guy," he whispered. "Bad stuff." I'd heard it too. Kieran had only arrived at school yesterday, but there were already rumors about why he'd transferred from another school in the middle of term. Everybody knows that gossip is vicious in high school. But these rumors were bad even when you accounted for exaggeration. My friend Graham had said he'd heard that Kieran had hit a teacher at his last school. Someone else had said he'd started a fire in a chem lab.

You could tell that the teachers knew something was up with this kid. Mr. Kurtzia was looking at Kieran like he was an animal that might bite if you got too close. Then I realized Mr. Kurtzia had led Kieran over to our lab bench.

"Taylor, I want you to take Kieran around for his first day. You know, show him how things work. Asha, how about you join Jake for today's lab?"

Trapped. I just nodded at Mr. Kurtzia. This day was going downhill for me, fast. Asha piled up her books and moved away. She didn't look back.

"Kieran, listen to Taylor," continued Mr. Kurtzia, turning to head back to his desk. "You can learn a lot from him— he's a good kid."

Kieran looked me dead in the eye. His eyes were weird, a pale light blue like a husky dog.

Sitting down, he checked out the dissection on the table. Then he passed the scalpel to me.

"I'm not doing this," he said. "You cut. I'll watch."

"Yeah, well, I think you get the honor," I said. "As the new guy."

"Whatever."

"Fine."

Kieran and I sat with our arms crossed, staring at the mangled thing on the dissection plate. Neither one of us moved. After few minutes, Mr. Kurtzia noticed and came back over. He looked concerned.

"What seems to be the matter, gentlemen?" he asked. "Is Kieran causing a problem?" Before I could answer, Kieran slammed his palm on the table.

"What the hell?" he said.

"That language isn't acceptable in my—," Mr. Kurtzia started to say. But Kieran cut in.

"You assume that I'm the problem? How long have I been in your classroom? What, ten whole minutes? Have you even given me a chance?" Kieran's voice rose in volume. His face had gone all tight and white, his blue eyes squinting with rage. Then he stood up, spilling the stool over behind him.

"Right now, you clearly *are* the problem. Calm down. *Now*," said Mr. Kurtzia.

"I won't calm down! This is the same old shit as my old school," shouted Kieran. "Screw you! I don't need any of this." Kieran dropped back into his seat. There was a sudden silence. Mr. Kurtzia took off his glasses and rubbed them slowly on his sweater.

"Kieran, walk with me," he said. "We're going to visit the principal. Now."

Chapter Three

Mr. Kurtzia still hadn't returned by the time the bell rang. I packed up my binders and grabbed my backpack. I was about to leave when I realized that Kieran had left his cell phone on the bench. I picked it up and held the phone for a second, thinking about what to do. While I was holding it, I accidentally brushed the screen and turned it on.

The screen showed a familiar website. Citycrawler.net was where I uploaded all my urban exploration photos. In fact, one of my photos from the other night at the Orpheus was featured on the homepage.

It wasn't until the end of last period that I eventually found Kieran's locker. He was there, pulling his books and jacket out just as I arrived.

"Hey. This is yours," I said. Kieran looked relieved as I handed over the phone.

"Thanks, man." He stared down at the phone. "Listen, about what I said back in the classroom. I kind of lose it sometimes."

"Whatever," I said. "Must be kind of hard being the new guy." Kieran just shrugged his shoulders.

"Yeah, except I'm not allowed to be new. It's the same old shit, same old reputation following me around."

He closed and snapped shut the locker. We started walking toward the school exit.

"I don't want to get into your business," I said, "but I saw that you left this website, Citycrawler, open on your phone."

"Yeah?"

"It's an awesome site. I'm on there all the time."

"You?" said Kieran. "Weird."

"Why is it weird?" I asked. We had reached my locker. I undid the lock and put my books away.

"Don't take this the wrong way, but you seem too *nice* to be breaking into buildings."

"Well," I said, "there's more to me than you think, I guess. Catch you later." I slammed my locker shut and started to walk away.

"Hold up," said Kieran.

I stopped and turned back. Students flowed around us like a noisy human river.

"I just wanted to ask," he said, "what's your username on Citycrawler?"

"Urbex604. You got one?"

"Wait—you? You're Urbex604?" Kieran looked both amused and a little shocked. "You're a legend. I heard about you even before I moved here. You've gotten into everything. You did the Orpheus the other night, right? Those pictures were awesome."

I didn't normally like talking too much about this stuff at school. But Kieran seemed like he was genuinely impressed. And I felt kind of bad about the scene in biology class. Maybe I had helped get him into trouble with the teacher—even though Kieran had totally gone ballistic. Still, I owed him a chance.

"Why don't you come over to my place after school? There's more stuff from the Orpheus run that I never posted."

"That would be all right," said Kieran. He tried to pretend that it was no big deal, but I could tell he was grateful. I was probably the first person who'd actually been friendly to him at this school.

Later that afternoon I was waiting for Kieran in the backyard. Both my parents were at work, as usual. Mom had the night shift at the ER, and Dad wouldn't be back until he closed out the store around dinnertime. That was fine by me.

I'd taken my skateboard out to the pool. We'd drained it last year when Mom had lost her other job. Dad said it cost too much to keep the pool going for the amount that we used it. That was actually fine by me. When they weren't around, I cleaned out the leaves from the bottom of the pool and got a little boarding in. It was my own personal skate park.

I was trying to get some air when I heard Kieran unlatch the gate and come in. He appeared at the edge of the pool. When he saw me he sat down, legs dangling over the edge. He lit up a cigarette, totally looking the part of the badass in his camo pants and black T-shirt. No wonder the teachers didn't trust him.

"Nice setup with the pool," he said. "If I knew how to skate, I'd be jealous." I let momentum carry my skateboard up and down the curves of the pool, gradually slowing down.

"You can try it out, if you want."

"I'd just make an ass of myself."

"Suit yourself." With a big push, I jumped the side of the pool, landed and then kicked the board up into my hands. I was showing off, although I didn't know why I needed to impress Kieran.

We went up to my room. An hour later, I'd gone over some of my greatest hits with Kieran. It was kind of weird to talk with someone in real life about this stuff. Most of the time, it was all online chat forums with people I'd never met. Until I had convinced Jake and Asha to start coming with me, I was pretty used to being a one-man show.

I liked being able to trade stories with Kieran. Before he moved here, Kieran had been into urban exploration as well. I'd never come across him online, but if what he said was true, he had done some cool things. The best was his story of getting into an abandoned wing of an old hospital. He said everything was still there, like all the doctors and patients had just walked away one day in the 1980s. By the time I heard my dad making dinner downstairs, I felt like maybe Kieran was all right. The rumors didn't seem important now.

Kieran was about to light up a cigarette in my room, and I stopped him.

"Dude, not here. My parents would kill me if they thought I was smoking."

"Right," Kieran said. "You're a good little boy, aren't you? Just with a dangerous hobby." We both laughed.

"That's basically right."

"Hey," Kieran said. "Let's go on a run together. The Harborhead Bridge, tomorrow night. We'll start from the marina, go all the way up."

Okay, that sounded interesting. I'd explored the bridge before but never tried to climb it from the bottom. I could bring my ropes and climbing gear, show him some of the moves I'd been practicing at the climbing gym.

"Awesome," I agreed.

"One more thing," he said as he got up to leave. "Let's make it interesting. I'll race you to the top."

Chapter Four

The next night, I looked up at the bridge towering above me. I'd been here before. Harborhead Bridge was a dinosaur, really big and at least a hundred years old. It carried four lanes of traffic running over the bay. I'd spent a fair amount of time messing around here with my friends, crawling over and under it to see what we could find.

But I'd never climbed bottom to top, like Kieran had suggested.

Next to me, a big concrete column soared up to join with a massive nest of metal girders beneath the main traffic level. From where I stood, that main level seemed really far away. It must have been about nine stories above the water, because pretty big ships could sail underneath it. I could hear the gentle knock of the boats in the marina against the docks. And from way up, there was a steady roar of traffic crossing over the bridge.

I didn't see Kieran in the shadows until he lit up a cigarette.

"You know, you continue to surprise me," he said.

I walked over to where he was sitting and dropped my heavy backpack in front of him. The climbing gear inside made a muffled clank. "Why?"

"I totally figured you'd chicken out."

I rolled my eyes. "Let's just do this," I said.

"Not so fast. There are a few rules you need to understand before we play this game. First, the winner is the one who makes it to the upper room of the bridge tower first. You been up there before?"

"A few times." Well, once. The big concrete column that stood in front of us stretched up past the main level of the road, turning into a smaller tower that held the suspension cables. I'd been up there once but hadn't stuck around to explore much. The wind had been a killer. The well-lit ladders and metal-work leading up there had felt way too exposed to the cars going by below. I liked a few more shadows, a little less danger of falling.

"All right, rule two." Kieran stood up and ground out his cigarette with his boot. Then, with one fluid motion, he reached down and scooped up my backpack. "No gear."

He chucked the backpack into the dark, and I heard a muffled plop as it hit the water.

And sank. Kieran had a big shit-eating grin on his face.

"Game on," he said. He turned and took off around the side of the column. I stared into the dark where my back-pack had vanished. Then I pulled it together.

"Screw you!" I finally yelled, but Kieran was out of sight. There was a hundred bucks of my best equipment in that bag! I ran after him, sprinting hard around the corner. But I'd lost Kieran already—no sign. Then I heard a scuf-fling sound from above. He was already heading up the bridge column using a service ladder. But that ladder started about ten feet off the ground—how did he get up there so fast? By the time

I figured it out, he'd be too far ahead. I'd have to find another way.

I sprinted around the base of the bridge column and almost slammed into a small shed built against the side of the column. It must have been some kind of electrical room. There was a cluster of pipes and plastic tubes leading from the top of the shed and into the girders high above. All right, this was a start.

I grabbed the roof of the shed and pulled myself up. My hoodie caught on the edge of the sheet-metal roof, but I let it tear and kept going. Standing on the flat roof, I checked out the pipes leading up. There must have been a dozen of them in different sizes. What looked like giant metal staples held the whole mess to the concrete column. They were spaced regularly, a little thin and sharp, but nothing my gloves couldn't handle. Not a great ladder, but good enough. Maybe thirty feet of free climbing, up to where the girders began. Then I'd have more options for climbing, with bigger handholds.

My gut clenched. This was not my style. I was the cautious, methodical one. But my fury at Kieran burned through the nerves. Hand over hand, I went up. After about ten feet, my shoulders started to ache. I just hoped I wouldn't burn out before I made it to the girders. Once I was up there, I could find a place to catch my breath. Until then, I had to keep going or fall. Occasionally, I could hear Kieran somewhere out there in the dark above me.

"Screw. You. Kieran." I grunted, each word punctuated by climbing up one more rung of my improvised ladder.

Then I was there. I crawled onto a support beam and sat, chest heaving and arms shaking. Traffic rumbled overhead. Looking around, I could see

Kieran resting on another girder about twenty feet away. He looked wiped out. He might have given himself a head start, but he clearly wasn't as strong a climber as me. I had a chance to beat him. And make him pay for my gear.

My heart still slamming in my chest, I started across the metal girders like a tightrope walker. One foot in front of the other, arms outstretched. I didn't let myself look down, but the distant sound of the waves told me I was very high up. The girders were wider than my shoes but not by much. I was still unsteady from the fast climb up the column, and I started to wobble. I knew that I was asking for trouble, rushing like this.

It happened when I tried to transfer from one girder to another. Most of these metal beams had been pretty dry, but some grease or water must have leaked through from the traffic deck just above me. As I shifted my weight from one girder to the next, my front foot went out from underneath me.

You hear people say that in a life-or-death situation, time seems to go into slow motion. It didn't for me. Way too quickly, I slid off the girder, reaching out for nothing but air.

Chapter Five

I was lucky. Kind of. Totally off balance, both feet went right off the girder. Which meant that as I went down, I spun and hit the steel beam with my chest. I felt a flash of intense pain as all the air was knocked out of my lungs. Just by reflex, both hands grabbed onto the far edge of the I-shaped girder. But right away, my fingers started slipping. And I still couldn't squeeze in a full breath. I'd only delayed my long fall into the harbor. And from this high up, hitting the water would kill me.

For a minute there was just the sound of the waves, the traffic above me and my ragged breathing. The steady wind was making me feel cold and clammy. I started to shiver.

"Gimme your hand."

I looked up and there was Kieran, sitting next to me with his arm outstretched. His long hair was out of the ponytail and was matted with sweat to his forehead. He must have somehow spidered across the girders to get here. Now he was the only thing that could keep me from dropping like a rock.

I released my left hand and held it out to him. He locked onto my wrist with two hands. Slowly, carefully, we worked to get me back into a sitting position on the girder.

Now Kieran and I looked like two kids facing each other on a playground teeter-totter, legs dangling almost a hundred feet above the water. I laughed, kind of high-pitched and nervous.

"You think that was funny?" said Kieran, but he was smiling. "You're crazier than me, man."

"I'm crazy? You're the one who pitched my gear into the bay. You're the one who got us up here." Despite my relief, the anger started to seep back in.

"I saved your life too."

"Yeah. I guess you did," I admitted.

"But that thing with your backpack, that was an asshole move. I get carried away sometimes, kind of lose control, you know? I'm sorry." Kieran was looking straight at me like he meant it.

"There was a hundred bucks of climbing gear in that bag. I don't have that kind of money to lose." More than angry, I was just feeling sorry for myself all of a sudden. I was shivering pretty badly now. I was starting to hurt. Kieran was staring at me.

"Let's get down from here. You look like crap. Then you tell me how much you need and I'll take care of it."

By the time we carefully picked our way down off the bridge, it was about 11:00 PM. I'd told my parents I was hanging at Jake's tonight. On Friday nights they usually let me stay out until midnight. So I agreed when Kieran offered to buy me a coffee before I headed home.

We found a place that was still open. The sour-faced waitress didn't look impressed by our appearance when we walked in. Two dirty, tired teenagers in ripped-up clothes. But she took our order without complaint. We settled into a brown vinyl-covered booth at the back. I watched as Kieran dug some pills out his pocket, washing them down with his coffee. Kieran saw my look.

"Headache," he explained. "So money's an issue for you?" I was working on a donut with one hand and cradling my mug of hot coffee with the other. My fingers were starting to thaw out.

"It's not that big a deal. Both my parents are working now. It's not like we're poor. But, yeah, I need to find my own cash. And I don't have a job right now. Or anything lined up for the summer." That brought back memories of Asha. I was pretty sure she'd been avoiding me after our conversation in the lab.

"Fair enough. Like I said, I feel bad about chucking your gear in the bay," said Kieran. "Is this enough to cover it?" He pulled out a wad of bills and peeled off a couple of fifties. He slid them across the table. I just stared at them.

"Where'd you get that kind of cash?" I said. Kieran laughed.

"You want it or not?" he said. I did. So I took the money. Like Kieran had said, fair enough. He might act crazy, but at least he knew how to make things right again.

"You know, I might be able to help you earn some serious scratch," Kieran said. He leaned back in the booth and squinted at me. "Despite your slipup there, you were pretty awesome. I still don't know how you got ahead of me. I gave myself a pretty good head start."

"I've had a lot of practice," I answered. "My parents are always busy, and I don't have any brothers or sisters. So there's no one to look over my shoulder. Which means I've been crawling all over the city since I was, like, twelve."

"It shows. You're good," he said. Then he leaned across the table. "I want your help. I need to get in somewhere, and I don't know how to do it. You figure it out, and there's money in it for you."

"What, you'd hire me to be your tour guide? You messing with me?" I said.

"No, I'm dead serious," he said, dropping his voice. "It's like this. My dad works at a company called DMA. They do high-tech stuff for the military. Building drone planes, putting satellites together. My dad said that they even used to build rockets for NASA back in the 1960s. They used to be a huge company, but now they've cut back.

"A couple of months ago, my dad transferred to this branch of DMA. Then, after we moved, there was about a week before I could start school. So my dad decided to bring me to work. Didn't want to leave me alone in the house, he said. Like I needed a babysitter. Anyways, I was able to explore around some of the DMA buildings while I was there. It's like a small city out there, big gate around the whole thing. Here, take a look at this." He pulled out his smartphone, swiped at it for a moment, then handed it to me. There was a series of pictures on it—a bunch of big warehouses, clearly unused for a long time. The inside of some kind of lab, lots of wiring and computers, crazy-looking equipment scattered around. It looked like an abandoned mad scientist's lab. It looked totally amazing.

"So I had this idea," Kieran continued. "The company owns a ton of space with all these warehouses and labs. But they only use a tiny part of it now. Most of that place is basically abandoned."

"But your dad still works there, right? So it's not all abandoned. Doesn't that mean there's security? If it's military, pretty serious security?"

Kieran looked smug. He lowered his voice.

"My dad is the head of security for the DMA site. That's why I've got blueprints, plans of the entire place.

Everything we need to figure out how to get in."

"You stole them from him?"

"Copied them from his laptop to mine," said Kieran. He pulled out his lighter and started fiddling with it. "So what do you think?"

"What if your dad figures out you stole stuff from him?"

"Whatever. Forget about my dad. We won't get caught. It's not like he'll suspect me. He barely knows I'm around most of the time."

Kieran's cold blue eyes studied me. The whole situation seemed seriously sketchy.

"You just want to get in there to explore? It doesn't seem worth the risk," I said at last. I drained the last cold puddle of coffee from my mug.

"Well, I haven't told you everything," said Kieran. "This is where the money comes in. In these files I got from my dad's laptop, there was an email. The company is storing a bunch of stuff in one of the old warehouses. Crates of high-end smartphones that DMA was going to use for testing or something."

"So what?" I asked.

"So we figure out a way in. We bring a couple of backpacks, fill them up with the phones and stuff. I'll take care of selling them and give you half the profits."

I shook my head. "I'm not a thief. I've never taken a thing from the places I've been. No way."

"This isn't even stealing. DMA won't even know that the stuff is missing. And we could make five grand, easy." The number was a shock to me—that was a ton of money. My bank account had never broken a thousand, even when I was working after school.

All of a sudden, exhaustion came crashing down on me.

"I don't know. I need to think about this," I said. The coffee shop felt over-heated and damp. I looked at my watch. It was close to midnight. "I need to get home. My parents are going to freak if they catch me out this late."

"Don't sweat it. I'll drive you home. So you never steal and you always stick to your curfew?" Kieran said. He tossed some cash on the plastic table, and we left. His car was parked nearby, a used sports car, a little beaten up. We took off, Kieran accelerating hard. The way he drove, I'd make it home before my curfew. No problem.

"One more question," I said, watching as Kieran steered expertly in and out of traffic. "Why me? Why not just do the whole job yourself?"

Kieran stared straight ahead, wrist draped over the wheel. Cars blurred by.

"Why you?" he said. "Because you're actually as good as your online rep.

You're smart. You know what you're doing."

We were driving faster now, the speed pushing me back into my seat.

"I want to get into DMA," said Kieran. "And I know exactly how tough it's going to be. I can't do it alone. I need you, man."

Chapter Six

"Belay on?" I asked, my hands resting on the craggy plastic holds.

A couple of days later, Asha and I were at the climbing gym. It's one of my favorite places to go, and Asha was always into it as well. Things had been tense between us since she had told me about her summer job. I thought having a proper date might help sort things out between us. A proper date for us involved climbing up a fifteen-foot wall. I was about to head up, with Asha belaying me. I glanced over to see her holding the safety rope attached to my harness.

"Belay on," she said. I started up the wall. At five feet, I lunged for a big jug-shaped grip and missed. I fell back, feeling the safety rope lock tight. Damn. I wasn't focused.

Asha unlocked the belay device and let the rope slip through her fingers, dropping me down. When I was about a foot from the blue crash mats, she tightened the harness. I jerked to a halt. I was stuck like a fish on a line, dangling just off the ground. She grinned at me.

"Cute," I said. "You're gonna let me down?"

"I guess. You want to try again?" said Asha. She looked pretty with her long dark hair back in a ponytail. The tight white T-shirt didn't hurt either.

"Actually, maybe I'll hang out for a while like this," I said. "It's a nice view."

Asha laughed. All right, things were going well. Time to get something off my chest.

"Listen," I said. "We never finished that conversation about you going away this summer."

"What's there to finish?" she said. "You obviously don't like it. And I don't have a choice. I need the money for tuition."

"So it's just about the money?" I said. Okay, now this felt awkward with me stuck at the end of the climbing rope. But I couldn't go anywhere without Asha letting me down.

"Well, I guess not," she said. She coiled some loose rope around her hand, thinking. "I'm also kind of proud that I got this job. It wasn't easy. It'll look good on my résumé, and that'll help on my college application. I sort of thought you might be proud of me too."

Why would I be proud of her? I actually thought she'd come up with the worst possible way to earn money. But I was smart enough not to say that.

"I am proud of you," I said. "It's just that I don't understand how money can be more important than—"

"Than what, Bex?" Asha cut in. "More important than you?"

"No! More important than us," I said. "We're pretty great together, you know?"

"I know."

"Then how can you leave?"

"Bex, part of liking someone is trusting them. Letting them do what they need to do."

"And, what—you don't need me anymore?" I cut in.

"I didn't say that, Bex," said Asha. "For such a smart guy, you can be a real dumbass sometimes."

Asha unhooked her harness from the line and spun away. I dropped down onto the crash mats on the floor and watched her go.

Crap. That got out of hand fast.

So much for my great plan to fix things.

But there had to be a way for me to manage this. I was the one who always figured out the angles, who came up with the solution to the problem. Why couldn't I figure her out?

Then it hit me. If I did the DMA run with Kieran, I could make enough money to convince Asha to stay home for the summer. I'd give her all of the money, and she'd have her tuition. She wouldn't have to go anywhere until the fall. It was more extreme than anything I'd done before. Way more extreme. But it would be worth it. This was the way to fix everything.

I dug my phone out of my backpack. My hands shook a little as I texted Kieran.

I'm in.

The next day, Asha was still avoiding me in the cafeteria. I'd been watching her and a bunch of her girlfriends across the big hall. She hadn't looked over at me once. Jake sat down next to me. He followed my gaze.

"Hey, why is Asha sitting over there?" Jake said. "This is our table."

"I don't know what's up," I said. Jake raised his eyebrows.

"I don't believe you," he said. His big hands folded around a burger, and then he took a monster bite. Chewed. Waited. He knew that eventually I'd spill. He was right. It took about a minute.

"So we had a fight," I admitted. "About her going away this summer.

But it's all good now. I've got it all figured out."

"Bex, you're one of the smartest guys I know," said Jake. "But you've always kind of sucked when it comes to girls. Run the plan by me."

"All right, but this stays totally with you," I said. Jake nodded.

I lowered my voice and filled him in on what Kieran and I were planning. By the time I finished, he was mopping up the last of the ketchup with his fries. My plate was still full of cold cafeteria food.

Jake shook his head. "The DMA place sounds cool," he said. "Might be worth checking out just to explore. I bet no one has ever been in there before."

Bingo. Jake was on side.

"But, seriously—stealing phones?" he said. He rubbed a hand through his short brown hair. "What happened to 'take nothing but pictures, leave nothing but footprints'?"

I shrugged. "Guess I'm not the Boy Scout everyone thought I was."

Jake looked at me.

"You've never been a Boy Scout. You're just smart about risks." Jake leaned closer to me. "This plan of yours goes wrong, you'll get busted huge. Like, cops, jail, the works."

"It's not even really a crime," I said. "Nobody will get hurt. It's a massive company. They won't even notice the phones are gone. They've probably already forgotten that those phones are in the warehouse."

"Maybe. But what do you know about Kieran? He strike you as reliable? Think he'll save your ass if things go wrong?"

I hadn't told Jake about the bridge the other night. Kieran *had* saved me.

"And even if it all works out and you get the money, then what?" he continued. "Her parents won't have a problem with this? You think Asha won't have a problem?"

"What do you mean?"

"Handing Asha some cash won't fix things between you two. I doubt she cares about the money at all. This is about letting her do her own thing. Trusting her." Jake sounded just like Asha. He was supposed to be taking my side, not hers.

"Jake, why the hell was I asking you for relationship advice?" I stood up, grabbing my backpack. I pulled out my headphones and my iPod. "Just stay out of my way, all right?"

Phones on, tunes cranked to maximum, I walked toward the door. My music sounded like static with a pulse. I was sealed in a bubble of noise. I felt angry and sad and scared, all at once.

I was losing my girlfriend.

Now my best friend was against me.

I just wanted to be able to think straight. I knew I could figure out the right thing to do. The right way to pull everyone together, to get control of the situation. If I could just get all the pieces straight in my head.

I was out of the cafeteria and into the main hallway when I was suddenly grabbed from behind. Jake spun me around, slamming me against the lockers. He pushed my headphones off.

"What the hell?" I said. Was Jake looking to fight? Had I pissed him off that much? I felt a cold knot in my stomach.

"You're being an idiot, Bex. I don't know what's up with you. But you're my best friend. And that means that I've always got your back, even when your head's up your ass. You understand?"

I nodded.

"I'm coming with you. That's not an option. You make a mistake, you'll make it with me beside you."

I knew I should be mad at Jake for acting like some kind of overprotective big brother. But the truth was, I was relieved. I guessed that Kieran wasn't going to be happy about this. I was supposed to go see him tonight. Maybe I'd tell him about the new addition to our team then.

Maybe not.

I decided I didn't care what Kieran thought about this. If my life was filled with static, at least I had one friend with me to try and see through it.

Chapter Seven

After school, I had to take three buses to get to Kieran's house. It was out in a new development, one of a row of homes carefully designed to look old. I pressed the doorbell and heard a ringing far away in the house. Kieran's dad opened the door. He was dressed in a pale gray sweater and collared shirt. He had small pinched eyes that frowned at me.

"Are you Kieran's friend?" he asked.

"Yes, uh, sir," I said. "We're studying for the geography test." Kieran had suggested the lie to me earlier. Studying on a Friday night sounded like a weak excuse, but whatever.

"I'm Mr. Ridgeway," he said. He held out his hand, and we shook. "Come in." He turned and walked inside. Weird. He gave off the same vibe that Kieran did sometimes. It was like he was an alien or something, just learning how to deal with humans.

"I'm glad Kieran's made a friend," he said over his shoulder. "Since we moved he's spent far too much time in his room alone." I wasn't sure how to react, so I didn't say anything. We walked through to the living room.

"Wait here," said Mr. Ridgeway. He disappeared upstairs. I studied the room. The house was completely silent except for the hum of a fridge.

The living room was perfect, like a set from a TV show. No mess. No clutter. No sign of what the Ridgeways were like. Maybe they hadn't had time to really settle in yet. Mr. Ridgeway returned with Kieran. He looked like he'd been up all night. His hair was tangled, and his black T-shirt was wrinkled. He had huge bags under his eyes. He nodded at me. "Hey."

"Boys," Mr. Ridgeway said, "I'd appreciate it if you kept the noise down. I'll be in my office." It bugged me how he was looking at Kieran. Like he was something that smelled bad.

Kieran didn't reply. We waited until his dad left.

A few minutes later we were upstairs in Kieran's room. Like the living room, it looked as if it came straight from a furniture store. A cheap generic poster of a sailboat was neatly framed on one wall. The single bed was perfectly made up.

Looking at Kieran, I guessed that he hadn't slept in it recently.

"Dude," I said. "You have the cleanest room I've ever seen. Do you actually live here or just visit?" I was trying to make a joke, but Kieran didn't smile. He slumped into an office chair beside an empty wooden desk.

"It doesn't feel like my room," he said. "When we moved here, my dad paid someone to decorate the house. He bought everything new and left all our old stuff behind. I think he might have left me behind as well if he could have." Kieran pulled out a battered black laptop from under the desk. "Doesn't matter. I'm not planning on staying here for too long." He jammed a memory stick into the laptop and typed.

I looked out the bedroom window at the sun setting behind the identical houses marching down the street, like an army of clones. This wasn't a place

I would want to stay in either. Before I could ask any more questions, Kieran spun the laptop around so I could see the screen.

"Here," he said. "Like I said, I've got a bunch of blueprints and maps of the DMA site in here. It's not complete. My dad nearly busted me copying this stuff off his computer, so I had to rush it. But there was enough for me to see that there's no way in. That I could find."

I sat down on the bed, taking his laptop with me. As I scrolled through the computer files, the screen filled with digital pictures and maps. I realized that this was going to be like breaking into a bank. There were security cameras, fences, guard posts—the works. Instead of getting frustrated, though, I was getting more excited. It was a puzzle waiting to be cracked. Kieran watched over my shoulder.

"You know, there are rumors about you at school," I said to him, while I worked my way through the files. "Did you guys move here because of something you did?"

I turned and saw Kieran's face tighten up. It looked the same as when he screamed at Mr. Kurtzia in the science lab. But he kept his voice steady.

"It wasn't my fault that we moved," he said. "It all started when my mom died."

My hands froze on the keyboard.

"What happened to her? Like, an accident or something?" It sounded awkward as I said it. I should have kept my mouth shut.

"No," said Kieran. "Suicide." I felt so bad for him right then. He said the word flatly, like it didn't mean anything. He stared at his hands in his lap, fiddling with a chunky ring on one finger. Then suddenly he looked at me, that hard look back in his eyes.

"I'm trusting you, right? You never repeat this shit that I'm telling you, get it?" I just nodded. Kieran went back to looking at his ring.

"I had a hard time with it. But my dad..." Kieran's voice trailed off. "My dad wanted to pretend that nothing had happened, like we had to hide her death or something. I couldn't talk about it with him." Kieran's voice was changing as he got more wound up. But instead of yelling, he dropped his voice almost to a hiss. Low. Spooky.

"He's so useless," he spat, his fists clenching. "You know something? When my mom got...sick, before she did it, you know what my dad did?" A vein throbbed near Kieran's temple as he spoke. "He worked more. Longer hours, always at the lab. Every night. He couldn't face her. Or me." His voice shook. "When things got tough, he made my mom disappear."

He looked out the window. It was like he was trying to get ahold of himself.

I waited.

"And after Mom died," he continued, "he tried to do the same thing to me. After she killed herself, I was pissed off at everyone. The fake smiles, the pretend friends. I mean, what's the point?" He shook his head. "I wasn't going to play along with it. My father thought he solved the problem when he found a therapist who would put me on a bunch of drugs."

"Seriously?"

"Check it out." Kieran pulled out a desk drawer. He held up a half-empty pill bottle. "Antidepressants," he said. Another bottle: "Anti-anxiety meds."

I shuddered. Who'd want to drug their own kid to keep them from grieving their mom's death?

"Anyway," Kieran said, "we finally moved when I got busted for starting a fire in one of the chem labs." He shrugged. "Maybe I did it. Maybe not. Didn't matter. It was enough to convince my dad that a change of scene would make me forget my problems."

"Did it?" I said. He shook his head.

"That's the problem," he said. "My dad wants to forget her. Forget me. Make us go away."

Kieran seemed to pull himself together a little. Maybe he saw the stunned expression on my face. There was way more going on here than I thought.

"Look, uh," I said, "the idea of sneaking into the DMA site is awesome. But I can't—I don't want to get into something between you and your dad."

"It's not like that," said Kieran, shaking his head. "You just help me figure out how to get in there, it'll be an awesome run. And as a bonus we'll make some money. Plus, I'll be able to do something that really gets my dad's attention, you know? No skin off your back."

This was messed up. Part of me wanted to get up and leave right away, walk away from the whole complicated scene. I didn't want Kieran's problems. But I felt bad for him. I knew he didn't have any friends at school to talk to. Despite his strangeness, I liked him. Especially now that I knew what he'd gone through.

And I wish I didn't care about the money, but I did. The chance to fix things with Asha was too big to pass up.

I swallowed my unease.

"Maybe there's something here," I said. I pointed at a blocky map on the laptop screen. "This is where they used to rig up the rocket engines for testing." I flipped to an old black-and-white picture of huge concrete pillars and iron girders. A massive rocket nozzle was strapped to the top. I'd read about something similar at an old NASA lab in California on the urban exploration websites.

"Underneath those big platforms, they built tunnels and filled them with water," I said. "The water would help keep the noise of the rockets down. Kept things from catching on fire too." I explained that the blast from the rockets would turn the water in the tunnels to steam. The tunnels vented the steam out, safely away from the testing area. I tapped the screen to show a point well away from the fence line of the DMA site.

"See these marks on the map? I think this is where the old tunnels ended. That's our way in."

Chapter Eight

We decided that we needed to scout the entrance to the tunnels before going any further. Hopefully, DMA had figured that the tunnel entrances were in the middle of nowhere and just boarded them up. Worst case, they might have backfilled the tunnels with rubble. In which case, I'd need to come up with a new brilliant plan.

Kieran and I arranged to go out there Saturday night. I left a note for my parents saying that I was staying over at Jake's house. As long as I told them where I was going, and had my cell, they never seemed to worry. A fringe benefit of my responsible "nice guy" image.

I'd been putting off telling Kieran about adding Jake to our team. But I didn't have a choice now. Jake and I arrived at Kieran's house together. When Kieran opened the door, he looked at Jake, then turned to me.

"It's not a slumber party, Bex. What the hell is he doing here?"

"Nice to see you too, Kieran. It's such a pleasure," said Jake. It was obvious what he really meant.

"Jake's coming with us," I said. "We need him."

"You told him?" said Kieran with disbelief. I nodded. Kieran swore and stomped away from the open door.

Jake and I looked at each other, then entered the dark house. There was no sign of Kieran's dad this time.

Kieran was pacing back and forth across the living room.

"What the hell gave you the right to tell him about our plans?" said Kieran.

"It's my plan," I said. "And it's my call if we need extra help. Jake is good. The three of us can cover more ground than just you and me."

"We don't need him. We don't need anybody else."

"What's your problem?" said Jake. He lowered himself into an armchair. He looked absolutely cool and calm. Jake was a rock. "You worried about your money? Because I don't want any of the take. I'm just here to back up Bex."

"What the hell? Are you serious? You're here for your BFF? What are you, in kindergarten?" snapped Kieran. He'd stopped pacing now. "And, no, it's not about the money. I don't give a crap about the money. Bex is the only one who seems to really care about that." He spun to face me. What the hell did that mean?

"Let me break it down for you," Kieran said. "I don't know if you figured this out, but we're committing a crime. You get that? We are breaking into a 'secure facility.' And then stealing stuff. We're criminals. And criminals don't invite their besties along for the ride." He pointed a finger at me. "You and me are the entire team, end of story."

I shook my head. "Not anymore."

"Bex, grow up, leave your buddy here behind and join the big leagues!" Kieran said, eyes bright with anger.

Jake looked at me calmly from the armchair. It was up to me. For the first time in a long while, the decision I had to make was clear. I dropped down into the other overstuffed armchair, facing Jake.

"How about I break it down for you, Kieran?" I said. "You said you can't get in there without me? I don't do this without Jake. It's that simple." Kieran just stood there, chest heaving.

"So, you want to try this alone?" I said. "Or do you want some help?"

Kieran looked like he was about to explode, go mental on me. But he held it together and took a deep, ragged breath.

"Fine. Whatever," he hissed. "Just get me in there."

Kieran drove fast, slaloming between cars on the highway. The glow of the city was behind us, the dark city limits ahead. The DMA site was less than forty-five minutes away from the city center. But it felt like I was heading off the map, away from everything that I knew.

I pulled out my phone and sent a text to Asha.

I'll make everything all right again,
I texted. **Promise.**

I hit the Send key, then put the phone back in my jacket pocket. The rest of the ride, I waited for the vibration from the phone that might be Asha texting back. But I felt nothing.

It was a warm spring night. The full moon was bright enough for us to see, even without our headlamps. We left the car by the side of a dirt road and picked our way through the thin woods on the edge of the DMA facility. The only sound was the hollow roar of traffic on the highway in the distance.

I'd taken some maps we needed from Kieran's laptop and dumped them onto my smartphone. The maps were pretty good, and I was able to quickly lead us to where I thought the tunnel entrance might be. Then it was a matter of hunting around to actually find them in all the bushes and undergrowth. After about an hour, I was starting to get cold. Then I heard a low whistle from Jake.

Kieran and I arrived at the same time. Jake was pulling overgrown blackberry bushes from a huge round metal grate made of thick rebar. It was set into the slope of a hill that rose gently toward the DMA facility, about half a mile away.

The metal bars of the grate were about the thickness of my finger. I clicked on my headlamp and shined it in. All I could see were the concrete sides of a tunnel, heading off into murky shadows. I flicked on my phone, activated the GPS and checked the digital map on the screen.

"This would make sense," I said. "This is it." I saw Kieran smile in the faint moonlight. All that stopped us from lifting the grate aside was some thin wire attached to the concrete. Jake snapped that with bolt cutters. Then we all grabbed part of the grate.

"On the count of three," I said. It was heavy, almost too heavy to move. We grunted and heaved. The grate finally flipped away from the tunnel entrance onto the ground. It made a ringing sound that quickly died away. Just the same, we turned off the headlamps right away. I scanned the moonlit darkness around us to make sure no one heard. There was no sign of anything, just a bit of wind rustling the leaves.

We went in.

The tunnel was big enough that I could stand up and stretch out my arms, no problem. But that didn't make it easy to travel through. The floor and walls were curved and slimy. There was a steady stream of knee-deep water running down the middle of the big concrete tube. I tried to stay to one side but kept slipping and landing in the stream, swearing at the shock of the cold water every time.

Occasionally there was a weird gust of damp wind like the tunnel was taking a deep breath. Single file, we kept marching through the tunnel in silence.

Fifteen minutes later the only thing different was that the stream was deeper, up to our waists. The water was cold, but we got used to it. The deeper it was, though, the harder it was to push against the current. To keep me going, I kept thinking about Asha. What she'd say when I gave her the money. What we could do in the summer, the places we could explore together.

We were all getting tired and cold. I wasn't sure how much farther we could go on tonight. I was pretty sure we'd have to turn back. We hadn't brought the right gear for something this wet. Beyond bolt cutters and a few other basic tools, we hadn't brought anything serious.

"Kieran," I finally said. "Kieran!" I saw his headlamp stop up ahead in the tunnel, then spin around toward me.

"What?"

"We need to go back and take another run at this tomorrow. The water's getting deeper, we need different equipment. I'm not even sure if this tunnel is going the right way."

"Can't you check the map on your phone?"

"No. The GPS doesn't work underground."

"Hey." Jake had slogged back toward us as well. "Did you guys see that?"

"What?" said Kieran.

"Turn off your headlamps, then look up ahead." We did. At first, the darkness was complete. The gurgle of water around us sounded louder than ever.

Then, faintly, a circle of moonlight appeared, way up ahead.

"That's the exit to DMA!" shouted Kieran. "Let's go!" With new energy, we splashed up the tunnel.

We were exhausted and not thinking straight. We were sloppy. So when things went wrong, we were totally unprepared for it.

It started with a slight splash up ahead, almost like a small rock dropping in the water. I didn't think anything of it. It took me a second to realize that the light from Jake's headlamp had disappeared.

"Jake!" I screamed. Kieran spun around to face me, then back toward where Jake had been a second ago. We both shouted his name.

But he was gone.

Chapter Nine

I shoved Kieran to one side, and surged
forward along the tunnel toward where
Jake had been. What the hell had
happened? How could he just disappear?

Beneath the water, I felt a hand grip
my ankle.

And pull me under.

Cold water pressed against me as
I went down. I kicked and thrashed.

But I was being pulled into some kind of underwater pit.

And then, just as quickly, I was being yanked back to the surface. Kieran had reached down and gotten hold of me. By the time my face broke the surface, I had figured out what was going on. I gulped in some air.

"Let go of me!" I said. "Jake's down there!"

Taking a final breath, I shook off Kieran and sank down again into the pit. It must have been some kind of drain tube, heading vertically down from the main tunnel. There was a small but steady current pulling at me as I dropped down four or five feet. When I hit bottom, I thrashed around. I could feel pieces of garbage, scraps of metal and torn up coils of wire. Then I connected with Jake's leg.

It was wrapped up in some of the wire. The more he kicked and tried to free himself, more entangled he became.

But I could tell that his movements were getting weaker. I wasn't sure how long he'd been underwater, but it felt like forever. I had to get him back up to the surface. Now.

Fumbling around in the cold water, I reached into the pocket of my cargo pants for a wire cutter. I got it out, then pointed it down around his leg. I cut blindly, hoping I wasn't connecting with any flesh by accident. A couple of snaps, and Jake was freed of the wire. He started floating toward the surface. I pushed off from the bottom, trying to get us both up as fast as possible.

We broke the surface at the same time. Kieran helped me up, and together we half-dragged, half-floated Jake back down the tunnel toward the entrance. Jake was conscious. Coughing up water. But he was breathing.

It wasn't until we reached the tunnel entrance that I realized how badly Jake was bleeding. There were still pieces of wire wrapped around his leg. It was a bloody mess of torn jeans and steel. Like I've said before, I'm brave but I can't handle gross. I panicked.

"Stop," I said. "I'm going to call for an ambulance."

"No!" said Kieran. He looked at me across Jake's body. "You want to explain to the cops what we're doing here?" We kept going toward the car, Jake stumbling between us through the dry leaves of the woods. When we finally got there, we put Jake in the backseat. The bleeding seemed to be slowing down. I wrapped the leg in an old blanket, then put my jacket over Jake. He was shivering from the cold. Maybe from shock. I got in the front passenger seat. Kieran opened the driver's-side door but then stopped.

"We need to go back," said Kieran.

"What? Into the tunnel? Are you crazy? We need to get Jake to a hospital!" I said.

"Just back to the tunnel entrance. We left the grate off of the tunnel. Someone could figure out that we've been in there. Blow the whole thing," said Kieran. He was calm and focused. How could he not be freaking out?

"That is not the most important thing right now. Jake is hurt—don't you get it?"

Kieran didn't move.

"Get in the car," I said, "or I call the cops right now."

Chapter Ten

"You wouldn't. The Boy Scout would go to jail?" Kieran sneered.

"Try me," I said.

We stared at each other. Then Kieran swore and got into the driver's seat. We peeled out of there. Within a few minutes we were on the highway. But when the car hit the bridge overpass,

I realized that Kieran had driven past the exit to the hospital.

"What the hell?" I said.

"We're not risking the plan. We'll bring him to my house and clean him up. My dad's away on a business trip." Kieran stared straight ahead at the road sliding by.

"What if he needs a doctor?"

"Bex," Jake croaked from the backseat. "I'm all right. Your friend is a psycho, but I'll be fine. No hospital."

I turned to see Jake, pale and shivering in the backseat. But he tried to smile at me.

"This is going to be hard enough to explain to my parents. No doctors," he said.

By the time we reached Kieran's house, Jake seemed a little better. He said his leg hurt, but otherwise he seemed okay. We cleaned him up in the bathroom, covering the white tiles with mud and bloody scraps of his jeans. The wounds weren't too bad, once we could get a good look at them. His leg had gotten pretty scratched up, but none of the cuts were too deep. There'd been a lot of blood, and the jeans were trashed. But no serious injury that I could see. Jake didn't speak much the entire time we fixed him up.

Later, Kieran dropped us off at Jake's house. Jake went ahead to unlock the back door so we could sneak in. Kieran waited until he was out of earshot.

"Next week. We go in on Saturday night. Without Jake." I just shrugged. I didn't want Jake to get hurt again. Kieran nodded, got in his car and rolled off down the street.

The next morning it took some serious fast-talking to convince Jake's parents that his trashed jeans and new wounds weren't a big deal. We made up a pretty good story about climbing a fence to recover a ball during a pickup soccer game. Jake seemed to think that they bought it. I was just glad Jake was still covering for me.

The next week at school, I avoided Kieran. I think he assumed that I was still on board. That he'd been proven right about Jake. I wasn't so sure. Jake and I talked about it several times, and Jake was pretty clear where he stood.

"It's not worth it," Jake said. We were in the courtyard at school, tossing a basketball around over lunch. Playing ball with Jake was always a pretty even contest. He had height. I had speed.

"I know," I said. "But how else do I get Asha back?" Jake slipped around my defense and dunked. He turned back to me, panting.

"You kidding me? I told you before, the money won't change anything.

You need to talk to her, man," he said. That wasn't going to happen. Asha hadn't even looked at me this week at school. I didn't have a way in with her. No matter what Jake said, I was still certain that I needed the money to end this argument between us. Her only real reason for leaving was that she needed to cover tuition next year at university. I'd take care of that for her. All of our problems would be solved.

"Bex?" said Jake. "You're spacing out on me." He tossed the ball to me.

"I've got stuff on my mind."

"Listen, I get it. And, like I said, I've always got your back. So you do this thing with Kieran, you tell me when and where and I'll be there." I couldn't shake the memory of Jake underwater, his movements getting weaker in the cold dark water. I made my decision.

"I'm not going to do it," I said. Jake gave me a big wide smile and practically hugged me. It was only long after our game had finished and I was walking home that I fully realized what I was doing. I'd just lied to my best friend. Even if it was to protect him from getting hurt again, I'd crossed a line. And I wasn't sure where I'd end up.

The week blurred by. Saturday afternoon, I was back on the bus out to Kieran's house again. We'd agreed that the two of us would meet up at his place, pack up our gear, then sneak out to the site around midnight.

"Are you sure we need all this stuff?" said Kieran. He was looking over the pile of gear spread across his bedroom floor. I was cross-legged in the middle of it all, sorting.

"We want to do this right, we come prepared." That said, I probably was over-compensating for our disaster last time by going heavy on the equipment. There was a full climbing setup, with a long length of black climbing rope, carabiners, belay devices and two harnesses. I'd dug up a collapsible hiking pole from our garage—might come in handy finding that pit in the tunnel again. There was my pair of bolt cutters, and smaller wire cutter. We each had a full set of dry clothes for when we came out the other end of the tunnel. Then we each threw in some extra personal stuff too. Kieran put in four steel bottles filled with energy drink and a bunch of energy bars. I added a can of bear spray from my hiking gear, hoping I'd never have to use it on anything. Or anyone.

For me, the most important piece of gear was also the smallest—my phone. I'd copied every map, satellite image and picture I could find on Kieran's laptop—and some extra stuff I'd pulled off the Internet. The phone would help guide us through the site once we emerged from the tunnel. While I had worked out how to get through the tunnel and under the fence, I still didn't know exactly what we'd do on the inside to get into the warehouse.

Everything went into two black nylon backpacks. Then, there was just the waiting. We'd decided to go in after midnight. But by 10:30 we were both hyped on coffee and nerves.

"Screw it," said Kieran. "Let's do this now." Then we were in the car and outbound from the city, lights blurring by.

Chapter Eleven

The tunnel went quickly, now that we knew what to look out for. I used the collapsible pole to poke ahead of us until we hit the drain tube that had caught Jake. Kieran was a strong swimmer, so he went first. He fought his way up the tunnel against the current, holding one end of the climbing rope. When he'd gotten far enough, he got his footing again, then held the rope while I pulled myself over the drain tube.

Kieran had barely said a word since we'd left his house. The entire way up he seemed jumpy, constantly checking the rearview mirror. It was like he kept seeing something that I wasn't, or hearing noises that weren't there. I was worried about those pills he was taking. He'd popped some on the drive up here. They couldn't be helping the situation.

Eventually we reached the end of the tunnel. We were too tired to celebrate. At this end of the tunnel, there was a metal grate similar to the one covering the entrance. But this grate was attached to the concrete with hinges on one side, and a padlock on the other. I pulled out my bolt cutters and snapped it off. With a strong push, the grate swung open. We were in.

We were underneath the engine testing platform, hidden from sight by some high walls protecting the tunnel entrance. The platform was awesome in the moonlight, a towering framework of rusted metal and concrete soaring three stories up. It was clearly old and abandoned, overgrown with bushes. There was crumbled concrete scattered all around. I paused for a moment, imagining a rocket engine strapped to that thing, flames gushing down over where we stood, funneling down the tunnel we had just come up. The black-and-white photos I'd looked at when I'd been researching this place didn't do it justice. I thought about taking some pictures to post on the Citycrawler website. Nobody would believe that I'd gotten in. Then I realized that I didn't want any evidence of what were doing.

"C'mon," said Kieran. "Enough sightseeing." He was right. We pulled dry clothes out of the garbage bags in our backpacks. We both dressed the same, in dark hoodies, black cargo pants, black boots. Then we carefully closed up the metal grate, placing the broken padlock back together so no one would suspect a thing.

I got a bearing using the GPS and the map on my smartphone. I pointed in the direction we needed to go. Silently, Kieran and I ran across the facility grounds. We stuck to the shadows, clinging to the sides of big dark buildings. In the distance, I could see lights glowing in a few places. It felt like we were creeping through a strange city during a power outage.

I paused to stop and check the map. Cradling the phone in my hand, I tried to keep the light from the screen from giving us away. We were about halfway to our target, the gigantic warehouse that loomed up in the distance. The trouble was, we were on the south side of the warehouse. According to the information Kieran had given me, there was an old loading dock on the north side that we could probably break in through. So now we just had to get around to the other side of the warehouse.

I was distracted by trying to figure out the best way to do this now that I could see things on the ground. That's why I hadn't noticed the low, mechanical noise in the distance. But then the noise got louder. I realized what it was when I saw the headlights. A truck. A guard. Coming our way.

Chapter Twelve

We were in the open, exposed between buildings. The truck was coming our way, and there was no way that they'd miss us.

"Lights off," hissed Kieran. We both shut off the headlamps and ran. The ground was uneven, and we both kept tripping and stumbling. All the while, the growling of the truck engine grew louder behind us. Kieran veered to the left, around the side of something that looked like a massive metal radiator. With the radiator in between us and the truck, we sank to the ground and caught our breath. I peered around the side to see if I could catch sight of the guard. No luck. Then Kieran pointed up. There were a series of ridges up the side of the radiator. Handholds, not great but usable. We scrambled up about six feet, then carefully looked over the top.

In the distance, we could see that the guard truck had stopped. The engine was still idling. Then a searchlight mounted on the roof flicked on and moved back and forth over part of the fence.

"That's pretty close to where we came in," whispered Kieran.

"Not that close," I said. But as we watched, the searchlight slid over to the place that we had just come through. I stopped breathing. The searchlight paused for a second, then moved on. Had we succeeded in covering our tracks?

The truck started up again. Only now it was moving right toward our hiding place.

"Think we'll get lucky? He'll just go past us?" I whispered to Kieran.

The truck kept coming.

"I don't feel lucky," Kieran said. He dropped off the radiator and ran. He was headed across a wide-open patch of ground toward the big warehouse. I took off after Kieran, keeping the radiator between us and the truck.

We sprinted across together like we were racing at a track meet. Each second in the open meant another chance we could be spotted. The distance seemed to stretch out forever. I was sure that any second now I would be surrounded by a ball of light and hear the guards barking orders at us.

Kieran and I hit the side of the warehouse at the same time. My chest heaved for air, and I crumpled to the ground. I couldn't move until I caught my breath, even though I knew we were in deep trouble. This was the south side of the warehouse. The only possible entrance was on the north side of the massive building. Circling around would take forever. And we'd probably be spotted by the guard.

Kieran was starting to panic, looking for a way in. There were no obvious doors. The windows at ground level were boarded up with big plywood sheets. Some of the aluminum siding was loose. But when Kieran tried pulling it off, it made a sound like thunder. He stopped, fast.

Then I remembered something. I had copied the map of the DMA site onto the phone back at Kieran's house. But I'd also copied a satellite photograph onto the phone. Zooming in on a grainy picture of the warehouse roof, I looked for anything that might give us a clue about how to get in. I frantically scrolled around the tiny picture on my screen.

There it was. In the satellite image, it was only a dark blob on the side of the warehouse. But it might be a fire escape, something we could use. I looked up at the side of the warehouse towering over me. I barely saw it by the faint light of the moon. But there it was. A black metal ladder running all the way up to the roof. Only problem was that the bottom of the ladder was about eight feet off the ground.

Suddenly, Kieran hissed at me.

"What happened to the truck?" He was right. The engine noise was gone. I heard my heart beating in my ears.

A spotlight snapped on and splashed across the side of the warehouse just above us. Did they know we were here?

Or were they just on patrol, and we were in the wrong place at the wrong time? Didn't matter. Kieran and I flattened ourselves against the ground.

The spotlight moved across the side of the warehouse.

I thought about our options. If we got up and ran, the guards would definitely catch us out in the open. If we waited, we might not be spotted. Or maybe we'd be nailed by that spotlight. The way our luck was going, I didn't want to risk it. So the only direction left to go was up. Straight up.

If we could time it right, we could dodge the spotlight. Getting to the bottom of the ladder was the problem. I whispered my plan to Kieran. Then we waited until the spotlight beam hesitated for a moment, locking onto something near the roof of the warehouse.

"Now," I said to Kieran. He stood up, and I stepped into his cradled hands.

Then I stretched for the bottom rung. My fingers brushed the cold metal of the ladder. Pulling myself up, I hooked my feet onto the ladder.

The spotlight was slowly sliding back toward us.

Hanging on with one arm, I reached down with the other toward Kieran. He leaped and grabbed my arm. I pulled up, hard. It felt like my shoulder was going to pop out for a second. But then Kieran had a grip on the ladder. I scrambled up with Kieran right behind me.

We tumbled over the edge of the roof just as the spotlight flashed underneath us.

"Shit! Did they see us?" whispered Kieran. I shook my head. I didn't know. We waited for sirens, for shouts, for something. Then we heard the engine of the guard truck start up again and growl off into the distance. We were safe. For now.

Chapter Thirteen

We took a moment to look around. Now the night seemed calm and quiet except for our breathing. Gray clouds scudded across the moon, making shadows crawl over the rooftop. The huge roof was punctuated by skylights and ventilator shafts. Looking over the side, I could see a smaller building next to this one. It shared a wall with the big main warehouse. I noticed a few lights glowing in the small building. That was weird. I thought this part of the facility was supposed to be shut down.

I turned to ask Kieran if he knew anything about it, but he had slipped away. It took me a second to find him. He was bent over, working on one of the massive skylights. The skylight was the size and shape of a small greenhouse. Kieran was using his knife to pop out a big glass pane from the frame.

"Get the rope out and tie off," he said. The glass came away from the frame, sliding to the roof and cracking a little. I winced at the noise.

"We're going to go down through that? Seriously?" We'd just been chased by guards, climbed up the side of the warehouse. Now Kieran wanted to drop down on a rope? What was he, Batman?

"There's gotta be a better way," I said. "We were going to look for stairs or something, remember?"

Still crouched down, Kieran tied one end of the rope around a stainless steel pipe.

"I'm not going to break my neck falling through a skylight," I said. Enough of this Hollywood action-hero stuff. Then Kieran reached into his jacket pocket, opened his palm and offered me a couple of pills.

"Fine," he said. "Need some courage?"

"Your meds? Are you nuts?" I said. Even in the dim moonlight, I could see his expression tighten up.

"Then screw you. Go home. I don't need you anymore."

"Screw that. I want my share of the money from this. And it had better be worthwhile."

Kieran just laughed. "The big score. You really did this just for the money? You are just a little criminal, aren't you? What happened to all your ideals, Boy Scout?"

He took two of the pills and stuffed the rest back in his pocket. Then, before I could say anything else, he grabbed the rope with two hands and lowered himself through the skylight. I watched the rope shake as he slid jerkily down it. Pretty soon, Kieran had disappeared out of the range of my headlamp and was lost in the darkness.

Now it was back to me. I'd come this far. It seemed stupid to back out now. But Kieran was different tonight. I was into taking chances but being smart about it. Calculating the odds. Kieran was just going for it. Like he didn't care about getting hurt. Didn't care about anything except getting into this building. Maybe that was my problem.

Maybe I needed to be a little more like him, a little more radical.

Before I could change my mind, I grabbed the rope. No harness, no safety. I put my weight onto the rope and let it start to slide through my gloved hands. I dropped down, and pretty soon I was surrounded by the dark space.

The descent felt like forever. I figured I must be near the bottom, and my arms were starting to hurt, so I let the rope go faster. But I wasn't sure how much longer I could hang on for. I built up more speed than I expected and hit the ground pretty hard. I found myself on all fours on a dirty concrete floor. I looked up. I was in the middle of a vast, dark room.

Thick steel girders came down from the roof, marching across the huge expanse of the warehouse. Aside from those, there wasn't much here. Some garbage on the floor, construction waste, packing materials. I moved my headlamp, trying to find something, anything that might look like a crate. But the warehouse was really empty. It took me a second to realize what this meant.

There was nothing here. No crates of smartphones. Nothing.

Then I heard something on the other side of the warehouse. I ran toward it. Kieran had some explaining to do.

It was easy to find him. The light from Kieran's headlamp was bobbing around crazily against the wall. As I got closer, I could hear him muttering. He was so absorbed in what he was doing that he didn't notice me approach. I held up and watched for a second, trying to make sense of what I was seeing.

Kieran was standing in front of a set of plain double doors. They were faded and dirty and had a large chain with a padlock across them. Kieran was looking at a printout, maybe the warehouse blueprint we'd looked at in his room. But he'd made all sorts of scribbled notes on it. Then Kieran dropped the blueprint and smashed at the locked door in front of him with the hammer and chisel. That's what I must have heard earlier. A few strong blows, and the lock gave way, cracking open.

I stepped forward, calling Kieran's name. I was pissed about the money, but more than that I wanted some answers. Where were the smartphones? Why would he lie to me? When he heard my voice, Kieran whirled around. The hammer was still in his hand. He pointed it at me.

"You keep surprising me, Bex. Not in a good way."

"Where are the smartphones?" I said.

"You still don't get it, do you?" sneered Kieran. "There never were any smartphones. I just used that as bait. I figured you'd only help me out if there was money involved."

"But why did you need to get in here?"

"It's really simple, Bex." Kieran laughed, high-pitched and sharp. His face looked pale and sweaty. "I'm in it for revenge."

His smile snapped away like a light switching off.

"Now get the hell out." He pointed the hammer at me. I wanted to ask more questions, but that wasn't going to happen. I put up my hands and backed away.

"All right, I'm out," I said. "You're on your own." I kept backing up until I saw Kieran turn toward the door. Then I clicked off my headlamp and crouched down behind one of the big pillars. And watched. It was hard for me to figure out what was going on with only the light from Kieran's headlamp in the distance. But it was enough.

Kieran kept trying to shove the door open. Despite smashing the lock, it seemed stuck. Maybe it hadn't been opened in a while. Then I heard Kieran yell in frustration. He kicked the door until it finally cracked open. I watched him grab his backpack and push his way through the broken door. Now the warehouse was completely silent and dark. I crouched, trying to think this through.

I had a choice. I could follow Kieran, or I could bail. I could go right now, take off into the darkness. Leave all of Kieran's problems behind.

But I couldn't let go of the feeling that I was responsible. I'd gotten Kieran into this place. The way he talked about revenge didn't sound good. Against who? His dad was the only link to this place. That's when everything came into focus.

I ran toward the broken door.

Chapter Fourteen

Kieran was going to do something crazy. Something to hurt his dad.

And I was the only one who could stop him.

I hit the broken door hard, shoving through it like a linebacker slamming another player. I stumbled into a hallway. A brightly lit, clean hallway.

This part of the building was definitely not abandoned. I realized that I must be in that small building I'd seen earlier from the roof. The one that shared a wall with the warehouse. It was still a working office, with desks, computers. Security cameras.

Still running, I reached the end of the long hallway, where it split in two directions. On the right the hallway ended in a waiting area. Big floor-to-ceiling windows looked out into the night. To the left, there was a door labeled *Operations and Security*. A crack of light spilled out from inside. I wondered where the guards were, and how long it would take for them to show up. I figured we had a couple of minutes to get out of here. At most.

I gently pushed the door open. It was a huge office with a dozen desks spread across it. Racks of overhead lights were shining brightly. It took a second for my eyes to adjust. And then I saw him.

Kieran was sitting at one of the desks farthest away from me. His back was to me, and his shoulders were shaking. I couldn't tell if he was crying or laughing. "Kieran?" I said.

He spun around in the chair. His eyes were red, and his cheeks were wet with tears.

Kieran looked at me and closed his eyes. "Just leave me alone."

"Let me help you, man. What's going on?" I took a step toward him.

"Get back!" Kieran said. He'd gone from crying to yelling in a split second. "You shouldn't have followed me. You screwed up the plan."

"Take it easy. What plan, Kieran?" I said. Kieran shook his head, staring off into space.

I wanted to get over to him, try and talk him down. We needed to get out of here before we were busted. I kept thinking about the security cameras I'd seen in the hallway. We didn't have much time. Maybe I was imagining it, but I thought I could hear the wail of distant sirens.

"What was the plan?" I repeated. There were five desks between us. I'd have to keep him talking while I got closer.

"I needed you to get me into the warehouse," said Kieran. "Then I'd leave you behind and get into my dad's office."

"And then what?" I said. As I crossed the room toward him, I wrinkled my nose. There was a weird smell in the air, a harsh chemical tang. I saw the four steel water bottles Kieran had brought, empty and lying on the desk. It looked like there was liquid all over the desk. Even some on Kieran's clothes. From the smell, I was pretty sure he hadn't brought any energy drink in those bottles. More like lighter fluid or something.

"And then," Kieran continued, "I'd prove to him that all his work didn't matter so much. The big head of security, beaten by his own son. Look at his desk. Not even a picture of Mom. No sign of a family."

Keep talking, I thought to myself. Only two desks apart now.

"I just wanted to get in here and start a little fire. Leave my mark. Just to get his attention."

"Like at your last school?" I said, suddenly remembering the rumors about Kieran when he'd first arrived at school.

There was one desk left between me and Kieran.

"Yeah, but that one didn't work. Why didn't it work?" said Kieran. He was mumbling now, staring unfocused at the soaked desk in front of him.

"Then he thought he fixed me with those pills. But this fire will be different."

There were tears running down his face as he pulled out a lighter from a jacket pocket.

"This time the fire takes me with it," he said.

The lighter shined bright and silver in the glare of the overhead lights.

"Don't—," I said. I scrambled over the last desk, flying at Kieran.

He sparked the lighter and dropped his arm to the desk. There was a white flash of flame, and a wall of heat and noise crashed over me. The explosion knocked us both backward. The room was instantly filled with smoke and heat. Over the roar of the flames I could hear an alarm wailing in the distance.

I pulled myself off the ground, coughing so hard I felt like I was going to throw up. My hands were covered in dirt.

One arm was bleeding from a cut near my wrist. But I was alive.

Kieran. I found him half covered by bits of wood and twisted metal. Unconscious. The sleeve of his jacket was on fire. Trying not to burn myself, I struggled with his jacket. Finally I yanked it off and kicked it away. Kneeling, I quickly checked him out. His face and arms were pretty badly burned, his long hair singed. But he was breathing steadily.

There was a sudden whoosh from behind us. Turning around, I saw that the fire was spreading fast despite the overhead sprinklers kicking in. The water just seemed to make the oily fire spread faster across the room. Other desks and furniture were catching fire. I pulled my shirt over my mouth and nose, trying to keep out the acrid smell of burning plastic.

I grabbed Kieran under his arms and hauled him back the way we had come in. I hunched lower as the smoke kept thickening. My legs felt rubbery and shaky. I couldn't do this. I wasn't strong enough.

But we couldn't wait for help to get to us. We had to get out of here. Now.

I kept dragging, thinking, trying to figure out a plan. I remembered the building plans I'd looked over, where the exits were. Tried to think of something to save us.

The thick black smoke kept following us, covering everything.

Then I had it. That waiting room I'd seen, opposite the door to this office. It had a big floor-to-ceiling window.

It seemed to take forever just to crawl there. Finally, I let Kieran slump to the floor. It took everything I had to pick up one of the metal chairs in the waiting room. I heaved it at the window. The glass shattered into a million tiny pieces, exploding out into the darkness.

Chapter Fifteen

Two security guards found us outside, all cut up from crawling over the broken glass. I don't remember much of what happened next. There were red and blue lights everywhere. Cops yelling questions at me. Firefighters in yellow suits pouring water onto the warehouse fire. Then a medic taking me away from it all, shutting me into an ambulance.

I must have passed out on the ride. When I woke up, there was bright daylight streaming through the window of my hospital room. A nurse was pulling open the curtains. She told me that my burns weren't bad but that I'd inhaled a lot of chemicals and smoke. The doctor wanted to keep an eye on me. And she said the cops didn't want me going anywhere.

After that there was a steady stream of visitors. First, my parents. That went pretty much the way you'd expect. Equal parts worried and pissed off. In the end, I felt pretty bad about how much I'd shaken them up. But I didn't know how to make them feel better. Didn't know if I ever would.

Later the detectives came in. Two guys in business suits, short haircuts, hard stares. They made me tell the whole story several times and asked for a lot of details. I didn't lie about a thing.

I wasn't sure what they would do to me. I did know that it was time to just come clean. I wanted to set things right, change for the better.

But that night, I realized I needed to break the rules one more time. After the lights went out on the ward, I quietly got up from my bed and crept down the white tiled hall. I looked in each room until I found Kieran. But I didn't go in.

From the door I saw him sleeping, his bandaged hands looking like big white paws. His face was red and raw. Painful to look at.

Asleep in a chair next to him was his dad. One arm was stretched out, lying protectively across Kieran. I wondered if they would ever figure each other out. Kieran needed help. I hoped that his dad knew how to help him. I quietly turned away.

The next morning, I woke up to see Asha standing in the doorway. She looked scared and pale. I'd never seen her like this.

"You came," I croaked. My throat still hurt when I spoke.

"I wanted to visit you sooner," she said, "but my parents wouldn't let me. It took forever to convince them." There was an awkward pause. She finally came toward the bed, then reached out to touch the bandages on my arm.

"Bex, what have you done?" she said quietly.

"I'm so sorry," I said. "I just wanted to fix things between us."

Tears started tracking down Asha's face. She took my hand. It felt warm and soft.

"Jake told me all about your plan. About the money."

"He thought it was a stupid plan."

"He still does. And he was right. You shouldn't have lied to him about going in with Kieran."

"I didn't want Jake to get hurt," I said. Now I was the one who was crying. "I didn't want you to go away. I just wanted to keep everything the way it was."

"Bex, listen to me," said Asha. She sat down on the stool next to the bed, her face close to mine. Her eyes were deep and brown and beautiful. "As long as I've known you, you've always wanted to call the shots. Figure out the angles. Control the situation."

She kissed me gently on the forehead. "But sometimes you need to let go. Let other people make the plan. And trust that everything will be okay."

She kissed me again, this time on the lips. And I knew that she was right. Everything would be okay.

Sean Rodman is the child of two anthropologists who gave him a keen eye for observation and a bad case of wanderlust. His interest in writing for teenagers came out of working at some interesting schools around the world. In the Snowy Mountains of Australia, he taught ancient history to future Olympic athletes. Closer to home, he lived and worked with students from over 100 countries at a nonprofit international school. He currently works at the Royal BC Museum. Sean lives and writes in Victoria, British Columbia. More information is available at www.srodman.com.

orca soundings

9781554698455 $9.95 PB
9781554698462 $16.95 LIB

March has a perfect life: beauty, popularity, a great job, a loving family and a hot boyfriend. So when she discovers that her boyfriend is cheating on her, she is hurt and enraged. When she lashes out at him, he falls and is badly injured. March panics, flees the scene and then watches her perfect life spiral out of control. In a misguided attempt to atone for her crime, March changes her appearance, quits her job and tries to become invisible, until an unlikely friendship and a new job force her to re-engage with life.

orca soundings

9781554692729 9.95 PB
9781554699766 16.95 LIB

Tara's sister died a year ago, on the day that Tara didn't answer her phone when Hannah called. And Hannah stepped in front of a bus. Now Tara lives with the guilt of wondering if things would be different if she had been there when Hannah needed her most. Competing in poetry slam competitions is the only way Tara can keep her sister's memory alive and deal with all the unanswered questions. But at some point, Tara is going to have to let Hannah rest in peace and she will need to find a way to move on.

orca soundings

9781554698936 $9.95 PB
9781554698943 $16.95 LIB

Jenessa's a thrill seeker by nature. Anything fast, she's all over it. Angry and blaming herself for her best friend's death, Jenessa escapes to the sanctuary of her car and the freedom of the open road, where she can outrun her memories...if only for a while. She finds a kindred spirit in Dmitri, a warm-hearted speed demon who races at the track. But when Jenessa falls in with a group of street racers—and its irresistible leader, Cody—she finds herself caught up in a web of escalating danger.

orca soundings

For more information on all the books
in the Orca Soundings series, please visit
www.orcabook.com.